JAMPIRES

Jam for breakfast,
Jam on bread,
Lunch and dinner,
Jam in bed.
Jampires slurp up jam all day!
Jampires all say,
"JAM, HOORAY!"

All rights reserved. Published by Scholastic Inc.,
Publishers since 1920, by arrangement
with David Fickling Books. SCHOLASTIC
and associated logos are trademarks and/or
registered trademarks of Scholastic Inc.
www.scholastic.com DAVID FICKLING BOOKS
and associated logos are trademarks and/or
registered trademarks of David Fickling Books.
www.davidficklingbooks.com

First published in the United Kingdom in 2014
by David Fickling Books, 31 Beaumont Street, Oxford, OX1 2NP.

No strawberry jam was wasted in the making of this book.
David Fickling Books preserves the right for all readers
to get jammy fingers on this book.

Library of Congress Cataloging-in-Publication Data Available
ISBN 978-0-545-81663-2

10 9 8 7 6 5 4 3 2 1   15 16 17 18 19 20/0
                      38
Printed in China
This edition first printing, July 2015

Book design by Ness Wood

JAMPiRES

Sarah McIntyre   David O'Connell

For James and Treacle

FICKLING
d|b
David Fickling Books

Scholastic Inc. • New York

So Sam set a trap
before going to bed
and used his dry doughnut as bait.

In place of the jam
    he used ketchup instead,

then hid under the covers to wait.

In the dark he awoke to a hullabaloo!

First came

Slurp!

And

Yuck, ketchup!

Then

But what a surprise!
Was there **one** thief?
No,
two!

And their mouths
showed the glint of a
FANG!

"We're JAMPIRES!"
they said.
"JAM'S our favorite food!
We eat JAM! We love JAM!
It's the BEST!
We're sorry that all of your
doughnuts are chewed,
but we've wandered too far
from our nest.

And we both got SO hungry we couldn't resist
slurping from what we could find.
A dollop of jam would never be missed!
Or at least, we thought
you'd not mind."

"It's a deal," said Sam,
and took hold of their hands,
and they opened the window and flew . . .

...over rivers and oceans and strange distant lands,

and UP through the star-speckled blue.

And there in the sky, such a **huge** jar of JAM,
with Jampires in flocks soaring by,

above doughnuts that looked plump as cushions to Sam, and mountains of blueberry pie . . .

Over fields full of jam tarts, growing like flowers, sprinkled with white sherbet snow,

and castles of sponge cake with gingerbread towers
lit up by the ice cream moon's glow . . .

To skyberry orchards
where Jampire moms perched
under a sugar-frost dome.

So they thanked him
with doughnuts, the jammiest kind,
which they bring to his house every day.

And although they suspect that Sam wouldn't mind, they don't suck out the jam on the way!

"So where DO we find all the JAM we adore?

Well . . .